Uncle Amon

SPIKE THE DINOSAUR

Table of Contents

Hatching

Spike could feel an urge to move. He had never felt this urge before. He started to stretch his arms and legs. The hard surface that surrounded him moved slightly as he pushed and turned. Spike got his back legs into position and kicked at the hardened capsule. A crack! He pulled his legs back and sent another kick at the weak spot he had created. His foot broke through to a brand new world. It felt drier and colder. Spike wanted to stay in his safe, comfy shell, but he felt he had to move forward. Spike rocked forward and kicked the shell off one side while head-butting the other. He was free.

Spike's brothers and sisters were all waiting for him on the outside. All ten siblings were now free of their enclosure. Spike's mother started to clean the egg juice off his skin. Her tongue was long and sticky and it tickled Spike a lot. As she finished, she rubbed Spike with her nose and went to find food for her babies to eat. Spike watched her leave with amazement as he tried to understand this new world that surrounded him. His home was a nest of dirt his mother had dug for her eggs. The walls were mounded high and the little triceratops had to climb up to see over the piles of mud and rock.

The sky was so big and bright it nearly blinded Spike the first time he tried to take it all in. The grass was a bright green and the plants looked very pretty too. Spike was amazed when he saw a flock of Pterosaurs fly by. The large winged creatures let out a squawk so loud that Spike fell backwards as he tried to hide. Spike hid behind his brother, Charger, and it was a big mistake. Charger butted his horns on Spike's head and sent the little dinosaur reeling backwards. Charger was the first of the hatchlings out of his egg and so he was the biggest in the nest.

Spike got up and moved to the other side of the nest as he waited for his mother to return. The wind started to blow and Spike could feel the chill in the air. This was his first wind and as the gust left him, Spike wanted to follow that feeling. Where did it come from? Why couldn't he see it? The little dino-saur peeked his head out of his nest to watch the gust of wind as it moved trees and picked leaves up off the ground. The leaves twirled in the air before settling back on the earth. Spike looked in wonder at the world before him, he knew that there was so much more to see and do.

It's Time to Face Charger

Spike the little triceratops was only two days old when he tried to leave the nest for the first time. He lived in a herd, a large group of animals, and the adult triceratops all helped to look after the children. Every time Spike tried to leave the nest he was nuzzled back into his nest by his mother or one of her sisters. They would bump the little dinosaur with their noses until he was safely back in the nest.

"You must stay in the nest," Spike's mother would say. "There are very dangerous animals out there that want to eat little dinos like you." Spike's aunts all said the same thing as they stuffed the hatchling back into his nest.

"Let them try!" Spike would say and he would charge forward like he was going to head-butt someone, and boom! He would be stopped dead in his tracks by the nose of a fully grown triceratops. "I can take care of myself, whoa!" Spike would yell as he fell back into his earthy home. But even in the safety of the nest things were not that easy.

Charger, Spike's older brother, thought that he was in charge of the nest. "Everyone listen to me!" He was always yelling as he ran from one side of the nest to the other. Charger would run in smaller and smaller circles until all nine of his younger siblings were rounded up in the middle of the nest where he could keep an eye on them. Spike didn't like it when the grownups told him what to do, so he especially didn't like taking orders from his big, bossy brother.

While his other siblings calmly moved into place Spike came up with a plan. "Why do you get to be in charge?" asked Spike trying to flag down his rampaging brother.

"Because I am the strongest," Charger fired back.

"But how can we know you are the strongest?" Spike asked. "We have never butted heads." Charger accepted his brother's challenge as he came to a quick stop and squared up. "I need to start at the top of the nest." Spike said and Charger immediately tried to object, but Spike added, "If you are really the strongest it won't matter."

"Alright," Charger said, "But only because there is no way you can beat me." Spike ran up the side of the nest and disappeared. He yelled down to Charger that he was ready. Aunt Zelda saw Spike out of the nest and ran over to put him back. As Charger reached the top of the nest he saw his younger brother roll out of the way. Charger started to laugh until he was suddenly tossed into the air. Spike scampered back into the nest to watch his brother stagger to his feet.

All eight of the boys' siblings came running over to Spike, "How did you beat him?!" They all asked and they all cheered. It had appeared that Spike too Charger down. Charger was still woozy and didn't even know what had happened. Everyone was so happy, and they were not afraid of Charger anymore.

The Escape

After their epic fight, Charger became much easier to deal with. He started being nicer to his brothers and sisters and Spike and Charger became very good friends. The two brothers were inseparable. They ate together and raced around the nest. The one thing that they wanted to do the most was the one thing that they couldn't do. The boys were not allowed to leave the nest and head into the wilderness.

Just beyond the nest there was a patch of bushes and trees called "the wilderness" and the adults told the hatchlings that scary beasts that eat little dinos live there. Spike was not the kind of dinosaur that just wanted to hear things, he wanted to see these beasts for himself. Charger thought that he would have no trouble taking on any beasts that might try to eat him. So the brothers came up with a plan.

The little triceratopses found two large pieces of eggshell from the floor of their nest and poked eye holes in them with their top horns. The brothers put the eggshells over their heads and climbed out of the nest. They moved slowly towards the trees. Adult triceratopses had very poor eyesight and every time one of them looked toward the boys, Spike and Charger would stop moving. It was just after hatching season and eggshells were everywhere, so the adults didn't pay much attention to these new shells.

Spike and Charger crept slowly and silently towards the wilderness. When Aunt Zelda moved towards them the boys froze. Their aunt walked right by. The same thing happened with their mother and their Uncle Mort. Everyone was fooled by their egg disguises. As the edge of the wilderness got closer the boys threw off their costumes and ran as fast as they could to the cover of the brush. "I think we made it." Spike huffed as soon as they were firmly under a low hanging branch, but his brother was distracted.

Spike turned to see the beautiful forest canopy that had caught Charger's attention. There were so many leaves and so many different types of plants. The little dinosaurs had spent so much time just looking at their brown dirt walls that it was hard to believe a place like this existed. There were so many different sounds and smells. Charger took a bite of the fern that the boys were hiding under. "Euuyuck! These are awful and really chewy." Charger complained.

"That's because Mom always chews them up for us." Spike reminded his older brother. Spike took a step forward and Charger followed as the brothers ventured out into this brand new place. They were starting to get nervous. It was easy to be brave from the safety of the nest. Spike could hear all four of his knees knocking as he tried to stay calm. The triceratopses both jumped and spun in the air as leaves to the left of them began to rustle...

New Friends

The leaves were shaking and there was no breeze. Spike and Charger got low to the ground to try and hide, when a ball of brown and white fur came tumbling out of the brush. It was two furry creatures, about the same size as the dinosaurs. They were play fighting. Spike and Charger stood up and the fuzzy animals stopped to look at the new arrivals.

"Who are you?" The taller brown and white thing asked as he pinned the smaller one to the ground.

"I am Spike and this is Charger," Spike motioned with his horn, "We are Triceratopses, what are you?" The little animal had never seen such funny looking skin before.

"I am Claw, and this is my sister, Dot." Claw pointed to a small patch of black fur that looked like a dot on his sister's forehead. "We are squirrels."

"What do you eat?" Charger demanded to know as he lowered his horn and readied himself to charge. "If these are the beasts," he thought, "I know I can take them."

"Mainly nuts," Dot said as she fought her way free. She got out from under her brother and walked over to see Spike up close. "What is wrong with your head?" Dot asked as she played with Spike's top horns.

As Spike tried to answer Dot used the horn as a hand grip as she started to climb on Spike's back. Dot used his mouth as a foothold and she had nearly poked him in the eye as she swung herself over Spike's frill and onto his back. "You're weird," Dot said as she got comfy on top of Spike.

"You don't say that to strangers!" Claw warned his sister. "I am sorry, she is very rude." Spike tried to answer but the smaller creature's tail was dangling around his nose. Spike reared back to try and get away from it, but it was too late. He let out a very loud sneeze that shook his whole body.

The force of the Triceratops sneeze was so great that Dot went flying off his back and landed upside down in a fern bush. "That was awesome!" Dot yelled, as everyone watched her slip out of the fern bush and fall onto the forest floor. "Let's do it again!" Spike tried to run away, but the squirrel was up on top of him once again.

"Alright," Spike said with a smirk, "Hold on tight!" Spike took his new friend on a bucking bronco ride through the forest. They were just going in circles until Charger ran past with Claw on his back and they knew that the race was on. The young animals took off deep into the forest. They were having so much fun that they did not realize how far away they were getting from the safety of the herd and the nest.

Monsters

The four new friends ran through the brush, "Charge!" Dot screamed as she patted Spike on the back. They were gaining ground on Charger and Claw who had started the race with a bit of a lead. Spike was excited to be catching up to his older brother when all of a sudden he realized that he didn't know where he was.

"Where are we?" Spike asked, as he slowed his pace almost to a stop.

"Ahhh, the wilderness," Charger responded as he too realized that they had run very far from the nest. "Where are we?"

"Don't worry," Claw said, "That is our hole right up in this tree. If anything big comes along you can hide in there with us." The Triceratopses looked at each other, they didn't climb trees.

"We have to get back to the nest before something big comes along." Spike said as he started looking around to find something familiar, something that would lead them back to their home.

"What was that?!" A rustling in the bushes broke Spike's concentration and he backed very slowly away from the moving bush. Charger was frozen in place. Spike looked to see where their new friends had gone but all he saw was two tails disappearing up a tree.

"What do we have here?" asked a vicious looking dinosaur creeping through bush. He had long claws and sharp teeth, though he was not much bigger than the little triceratopses. As he walked closer more dinosaurs just like him appeared in front of the brothers.

Charger didn't move, Spike knew he could not leave his brother. He ran up beside his older brother and bumped him with a horn. Charger shook himself and the brothers started to back up together. "Where are you guys going?" The Compsognathus asked, "It looked like you were having so much fun, you should stay for a while." The Compsognathus took a step towards the boys and as he did a large nut sent him reeling backwards.

"Run guys!" Dot yelled as Claw launched another nut at the pack of Compsognathus. Spike could see at least five other squirrels tossing nuts from the trees, but he didn't have time to count.

"Thanks!" Spike yelled as he and Charger took off through the brush. The Compsognathus were thrown off by the airborne nut attack, but they soon fought their way through and began chasing the little dinosaurs. Spike could hear them coming through the trees. "Charger we have to go faster," Spike said looking back at the predators who were quickly gaining ground.

"There it is!" Charger shouted as he nudged Spike to the side. Spike was mad until he saw where Charger was pushing him, "Home!" The brothers yelled together. But they were not out of the woods yet, literally they were still in the woods. They picked up the pace and this time they knew exactly where to go. The brothers could feel the vicious reptiles nipping at their heels as they reached the edge of the herd and Uncle Mort. The Compsognathuses could not get stopped in time and with one big sideways head swing, Uncle Mort's large club like head sent the smaller meat-eaters flying backwards into the brush. The boys ran straight to their nest and laid down for a long rest. They had enough adventures for one day!

Dinosaur Jokes

Q: What type of tools did cave men use?

A: A dino-saw!

Q: What's the scariest dinosaur?

A: A terror-dactyl!

Q: What do you call a dinosaur with a large vocabulary?

A: A thesaurus!

Q: Which dinosaur can jump higher than a house?

A: All of them. Houses don't jump!

Q: Why did the dinosaurs eat raw meat?

A: They did not know how to cook!

Q: What did you call a dinosaur that keeps you awake at night?

A: Bronto-snore-us!

Q: Why did the dinosaur cross the road?

A: Because the chicken had the day off!

Q: What kind of materials do dinosaurs use for the floor of their homes?

A: Rep tiles!

Q: How do you ask a dinosaur to lunch?

A: Tea Rex?

Q: Why didn't the T-Rex skeleton attack the museum visitors?

A: Because he had no guts!

Q: What do you get when you put a bomb and a dinosaur together?

A: Dino-mite!

Q: What was the most flexible dinosaur?

A: Tyrannosaurus Flex!

Q: Why did the Apatosaurus devour the factory?

A: Because she was a plant eater!

Q: What are prehistoric monsters called when they sleep?

A: A dinosnore!

Q: What dinosaur would you find in a rodeo?

A: Bronco-saurus!

Q: What would you get if you crossed a dinosaur with a pig?

A: Jurassic pork!

Find the Differences

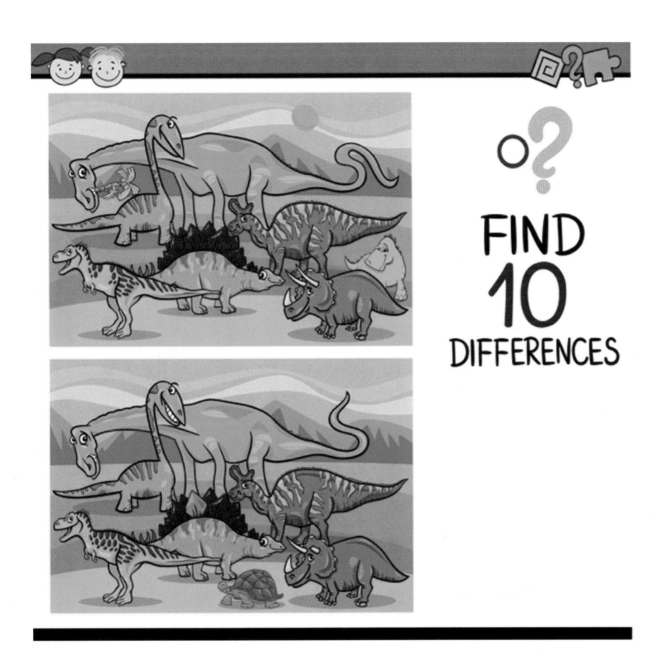

FIND
10
DIFFERENCES

Maze 2

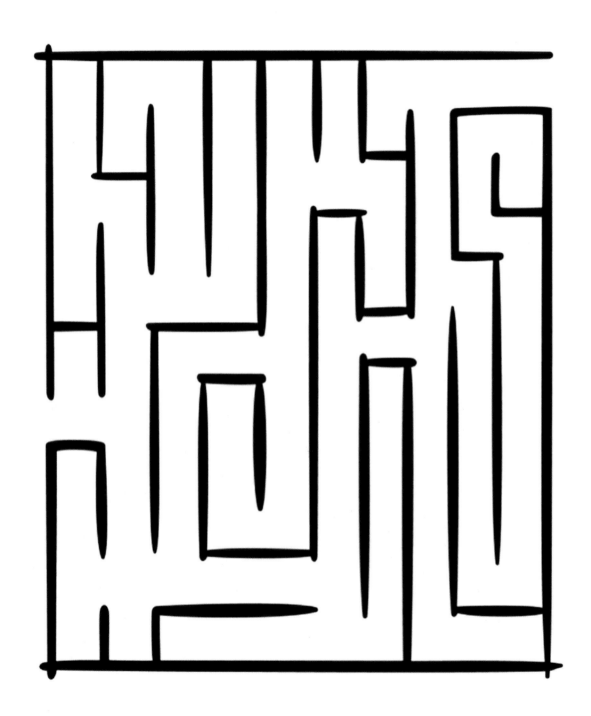

Maze 3

Maze 4

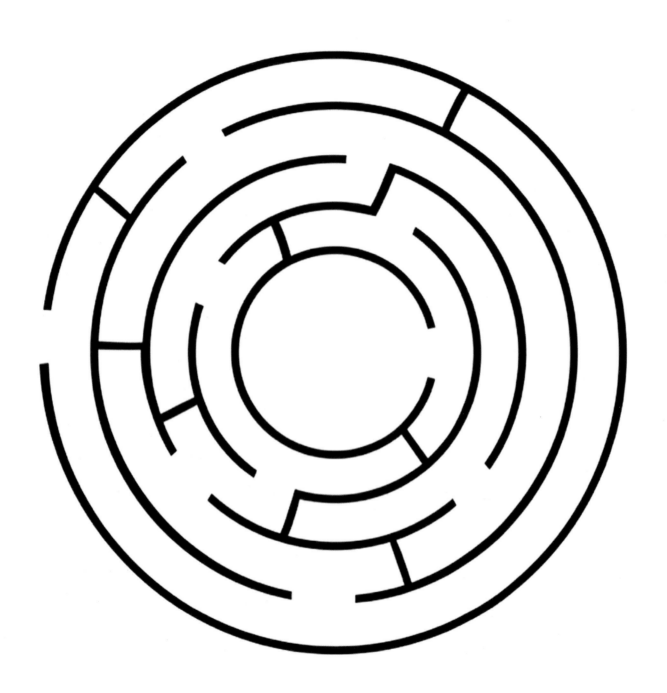

Solutions

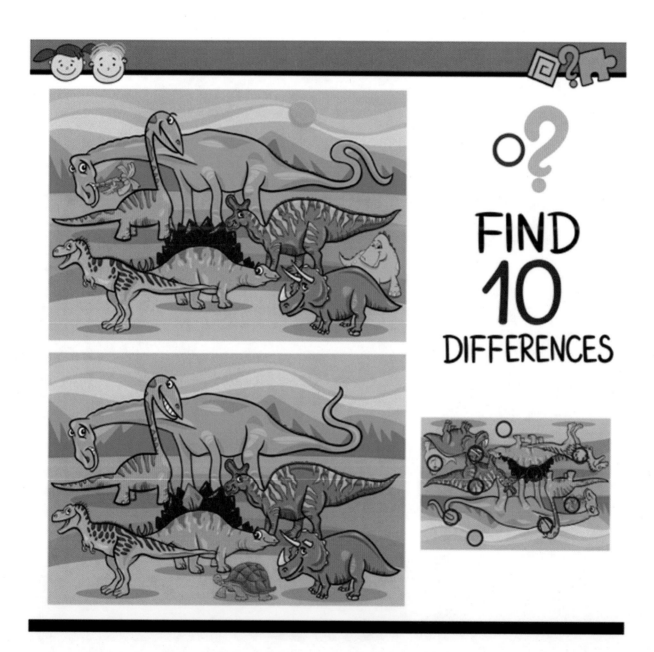

You will also enjoy...

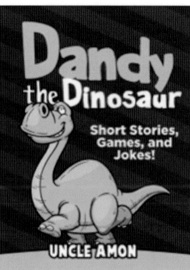

Made in the USA
Columbia, SC
07 July 2020